Ariane Dewey and José Aruego

SPLASH!

Green Light Readers
Harcourt, Inc.
San Diego New York London

Requests for permission to make copies of any part of the work should be mailed to the following address: Permissions Department, Harcourt, Inc., 6277 Sea Harbor Drive, Orlando, Florida 32887-6777.

www.harcourt.com

First Green Light Readers edition 2001
Green Light Readers is a trademark of Harcourt, Inc., registered in the United States of America and/or other jurisdictions.

Library of Congress Cataloging-in-Publication Data
Dewey, Ariane.
Splash!/by Ariane Dewey and Jose Aruego.
p. cm.
"Green Light Readers."
Summary: Two clumsy bears join in fishing fun at the river.
[1. Bears—Fiction. 2. Clumsiness—Fiction. 3. Fishing—Fiction.]
I. Aruego, Jose. II. Title. III. Green Light Reader.
PZ7.D5228Sp 2001
[E]—dc21 00-9723
ISBN 0-15-216256-9
ISBN 0-15-216262-3 (pb)

A C E G H F D B
A C E G H F D B (pb)

“Wake up, you big fur ball!” Nelly yelled. She gave Sam a shake.

“Don’t be a pest, Nelly,” Sam growled.
“I’m dreaming about fat, floppy fish.”
“Let’s go find some!” Nelly said.

Nelly rushed out of their cave.
Sam jumped up and ran after her.

“Is that sound a splash?” asked Sam.
“I bet it’s bears,” said Nelly. “Let’s
hurry, before all the fish are gone.”

Together, they ran to the river.

The river was full of bears catching fish. "Oh no," the bears groaned. "Here come Sam and Nelly."

“What kind of mess will they make this time?” said one bear.

Nelly slipped on a wet rock. She fell into the river. *Splash!*
“I’ll save you!” Sam yelled, slipping after her.

Splash again!
Together, Nelly and Sam made a wave
that tipped over ten bears.

"Why are you two always so clumsy?"
growled one bear.
"We'll be more careful!" said Sam.

“OK, OK. You can fish with us,” said the other bears. “But for once, try to behave.”

Sam and Nelly sat very still with the other bears. While they were sitting, lots of fish swam by.

The bears had never seen so many fish in one place. All they could hear was the sound of swishing fins.

"Quick! Get them before they're gone!" Sam yelled. Hungry bears snapped at the fish. The river was a jumble of fins and fur. The bears had fun chasing the fish.

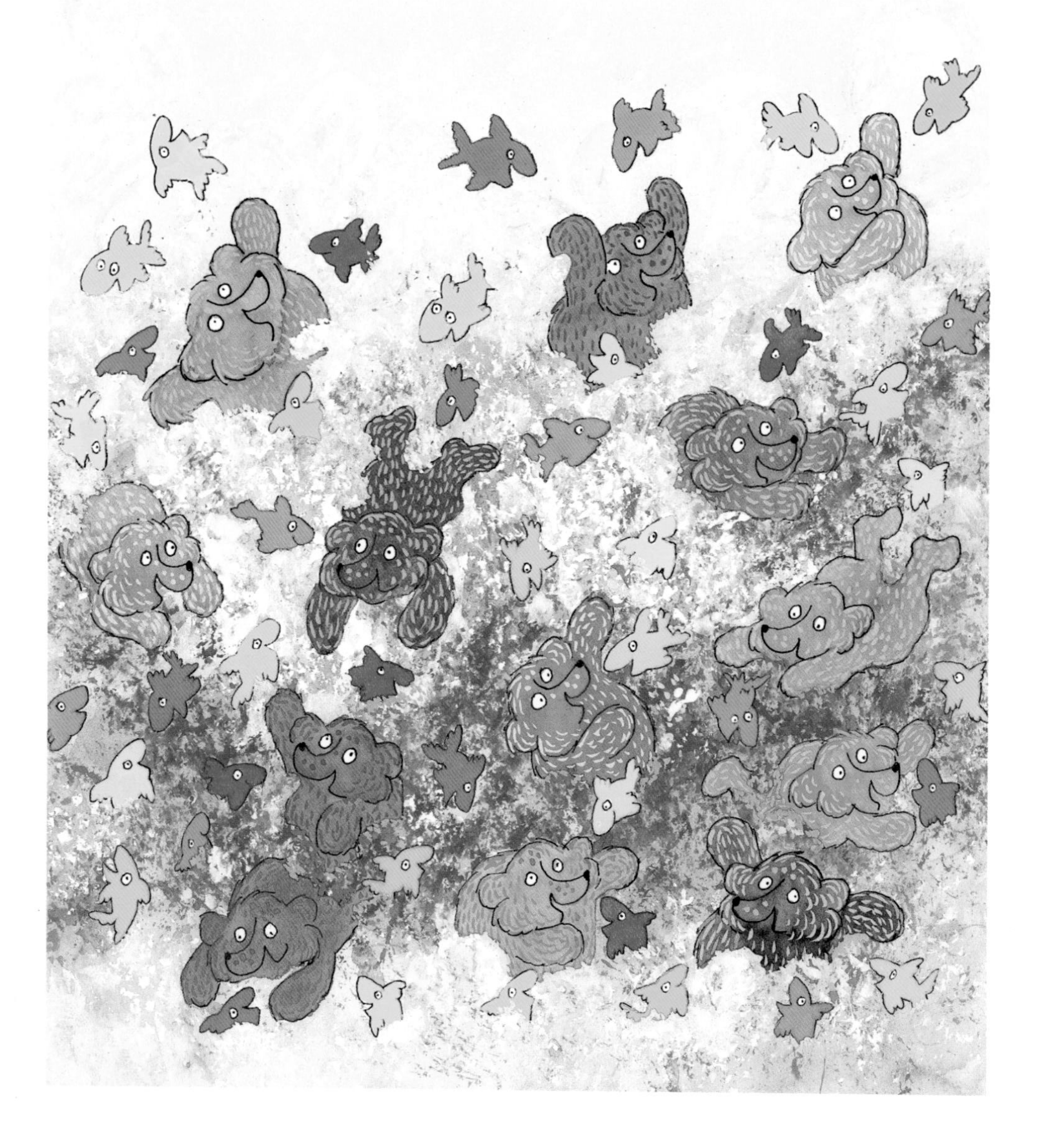

And the fish had fun racing away. They swam to the bottom of a safe deep lake.

All of the bears had so much fun, they forgot they were hungry. Sam and Nelly walked home to their cave.

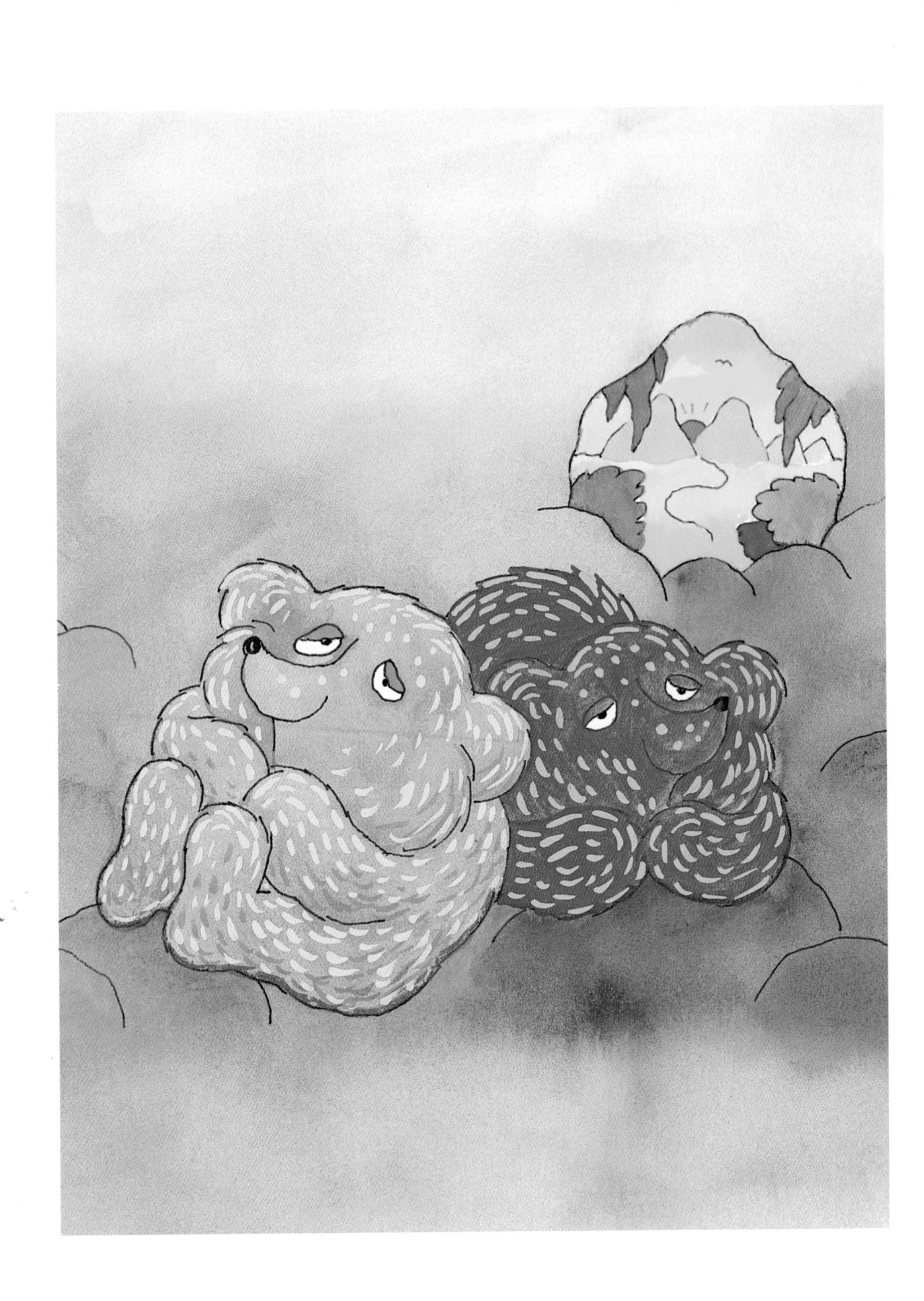

"We are clumsy," said Sam.
"But we do have fun!" said Nelly.
Now all they needed was a good
long nap!

Meet the Author-Illustrators

Ariane Dewey and Jose Aruego like working together. Jose loves to draw funny animals and Ariane loves to paint them. First, Jose draws the eyes. They show if the animal is happy, sad, mad, grumpy, or scared. Then he adds the ears, the nose, and the rest of the animal. When his drawings are finished, Ariane paints them bright colors. Ariane and Jose hope the bears in Splash! *make you smile.*